What a Way to Start a New Year!

A Rosh Hashanah Story

To my mother, who was a gracious hostess and wonderful cook.
Thank you for the holiday memories, Mom.

— J. J.

To Edie, for delightful holiday feasts, year after year.

— J. S.

KAR-BEN PUBLISHING
A division of Lerner Publishing Group, Inc.
241 First Avenue North
Minneapolis, MN 55401 U.S.A.
1-800-4-Karben

Website address: www.karben.com

Library of Congress Cataloging-in-Publication Data

Jules, Jacqueline, 1956–
    What a way to start a new year! / by Jacqueline Jules ; illustrated by Judy Stead.
        p.   cm.
    Summary: Having moved just before Rosh Hashanah, Harry and Dina fear the new year will be nothing but
unpacking and leftover pizza until their parents take them to synagogue where they meet the Levine family.
        ISBN 978–0–7613–8116–7 (lib. bdg. : alk. paper)
        ISBN 978–1–4677–1640–6 (eBook)
        [1. Moving, Household—Fiction. 2. Rosh ha-Shanah—Fiction. 3. Judaism—Customs and practices—Fiction.]
    I. Stead, Judy, ill. II. Title.
    PZ7.J92947Wh 2013
    [E]—dc23   2012027927

Manufactured in the United States of America
1 – PC – 7/15/13

What a Way to Start a
New Year!

A Rosh Hashanah Story

Jacqueline Jules
Illustrated by Judy Stead

KAR-BEN
PUBLISHING

It was almost Rosh Hashanah, but we weren't getting ready for the holiday. We were eating pizza in our new house, sitting on packing boxes.

"How can we have Rosh Hashanah here without the Kaplans?" I complained.

Dad agreed. "I'll miss Mrs. Kaplan's honey cake."

My father wasn't Jewish, but he loved celebrating the holidays, especially with our old neighbors, the Kaplans. Their daughter Lily was my best friend.

"Why can't we go back to Greenville?" my little brother Harry asked. "Mrs. Kaplan invited us."

"Good idea," Mom said. "I'll call her."

The next morning we piled into the car. Dad said he would join us later. Greenville was only two hours away.

Harry pinched his nose. "Marcus smells bad."

"He does," I agreed.

"Oh, no!" Mom grabbed Marcus from his car seat. "Let me change his diaper. I'll be quick."

Harry ran after Mom. "I forgot my special pillow."

A few minutes later, Mom came out of the house with Marcus in her arms and Harry behind her. **BANG!** The front door slammed shut. Mom grabbed the doorknob. "My keys!" The house was locked with Mom's keys inside.

"What a way to start a new year!"

Mom said, sitting
down on the steps.

We called Dad. He came home from work and used his key to open the door. Then we all left the house together.

I couldn't wait. In Greenville we had friends. In Greenville we didn't get lost on the way to the grocery store.

Unfortunately, we didn't get very far. **BUMPITY! BUMP! BUMP!** The back tire was flat. Dad pulled off the road.

"What a way to start a new year!" Dad said.

We called a tow truck. By the time the tire was fixed, it was too late to drive to Greenville, so we went back home to our packing boxes.

"It doesn't feel like Rosh Hashanah here," I told Mom. "We don't even have a round challah."

Harry opened the refrigerator and reached for a bottle of grape juice.

"Careful," Mom warned, but it was too late. The bottle slipped out of Harry's hands. Grape juice spilled all over the floor.

FRAGILE

"What a way to start a new year!" Harry said.

We heard Dad hang up the telephone. "I just talked to Alan Levine from my office. He invited us to join him at Temple Shalom. He thinks we will enjoy the services," Dad said.

"We'll eat when we get home," Mom said. "I have leftover pizza."

"No brisket? No honey cake?" Harry asked.

"What a way to start a new year!" I grumbled.

When we got to the synagogue, Dad introduced
us to Mr. Levine. He had white hair and a big smile.
"Happy New Year!" he greeted us.
We sat down just as the cantor began singing.
"It sounds like Greenville," Harry whispered.

He was right. The songs and prayers sounded just like they did in our synagogue in Greenville. But the people weren't the same. I didn't recognize a single face.

After services, Mr. Levine came up to us in the lobby.

"I'd like you to meet my wife," he said.

A white-haired woman held out her hand to Mom. "Do you have plans for dinner?"

Harry crossed his arms and pouted. "Leftover pizza."

Mrs. Levine smiled. "Why don't you come to our house?"

"Are you having brisket?" Harry asked.

Mrs. Levine nodded.

"OKAY!" Harry said. Everybody laughed.

Harry was satisfied, but I wasn't. One look at Mr. and Mrs. Levine's white hair told me there wouldn't be any kids at dinner. Rosh Hashanah would be boring, even if the food was good.

Then a boy about Harry's size came up and tugged on Mr. Levine's hand. "Grandpa!" he said. "Can we leave now? I'm hungry."

"Yes," Mr. Levine said. "But first meet our new friends, Dina and Harry."

"I'm Michael," the boy said.

"And I'm Maya." A girl my size came up beside us.

There was a large table in the Levines' dining room. Harry and I sat at one end with Maya and Michael. We ate round challah, brisket, and all the Rosh Hashanah foods we loved. Except there was no honey cake.

"My family likes apple cake better," Maya said.
"Try a piece."
"Yummy!" Harry said, taking a bite.
"Mmmm!" Dad agreed.
I nodded my head.

"What a WONDERFUL way to start a new year!"

Author's Note

Rosh Hashanah is the Jewish New Year, a time when families and friends celebrate with traditional meals of round challah, apples with honey, brisket, and honey or apple cake. It occurs in early fall, sometimes at the beginning of a school year, when young families move into new homes. Starting off a new year in a new place is never easy. But it always helps to be welcomed by warm and generous hosts.

The mitzvah of *hachnasat orchim* — welcoming guests — enriched my life as a child attending synagogue in a small town in southern Virginia. On the High Holidays and on Shabbat, my father always kept an eye out for newcomers and often invited them home for dinner. We made many wonderful friends that way.